VE BUNTING

TWINNIES

ILLUSTRATED BY **NANCY CARPENTER**

HARCOURT BRACE & COMPANY

Library of Congress Cataloging-in-Publication Data
Bunting, Eve, 1928–
Twinnies/Eve Bunting; illustrated by Nancy Carpenter.
p. cm.
Summary: A little girl gradually becomes reconciled to her new twin sisters.
ISBN 0-15-291592-3
[1. Babies—Fiction. 2. Twins—Fiction. 3. Sisters—Fiction.]
I. Carpenter, Nancy, ill. II. Title.
PZ7.B91527Tv 1997
[E]—dc20   96-7645

First edition
A C E F D B

Printed in Singapore

The illustrations in this book were done in oil paints
on treated Strathmore Bristol board.
The display type was set in Heatwave.
The text type was set in Cochin.
Color separations by United Graphic Ptd Ltd., Singapore
Printed and bound by Tien Wah Press, Singapore
This book was printed on totally chlorine-free Nymolla Matte Art paper.
Production supervision by Stanley Redfern and Pascha Gerlinger
Designed by Linda Lockowitz

To all my granddaughters
—E. B.

To my big sister, Leslie (now a mommy herself),
in honor of all firstborns
—N. C.

Last June I got twin baby sisters.
The worst thing is that there are two of them.

They need two cribs.
And two high chairs.
And two everything.
They take up all the space in my bedroom, in the kitchen. And in our lives, too, if you ask me. And they are twice as much work.

Mom says sometimes she feels truly overwhelmed. "That means 'swamped,'" she tells me.

Once a lady saw me. "Oh, oh. Somebody's jealous," she whispered. I folded my arms the way I do when I'm really mad. "My name isn't Somebody."

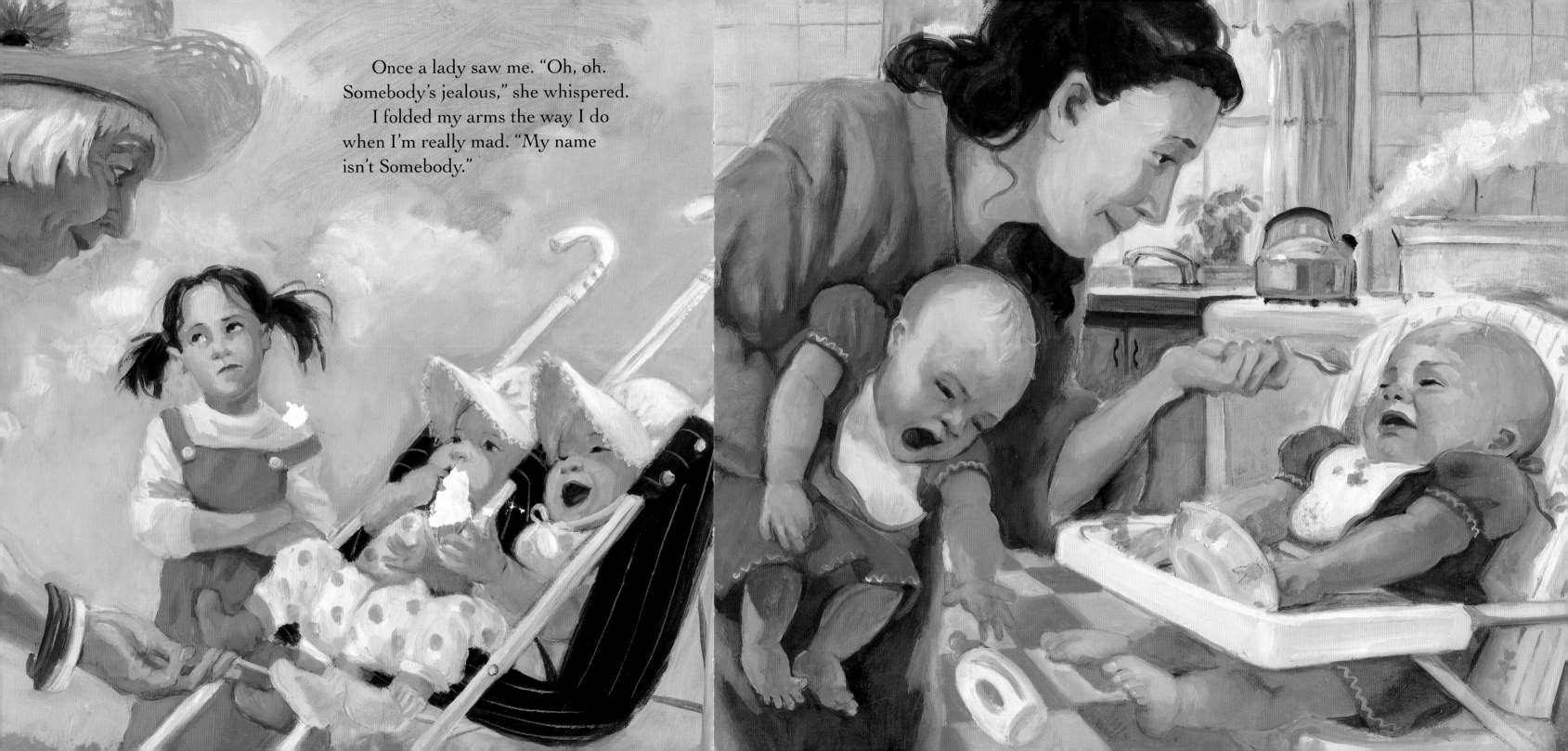

When we go for a walk, their stroll
up the whole sidewalk. People can't ge
They grin goofy grins and say, "Two of
Are they twins?"

Mom is polite. She smiles. "Yes."

But sometimes I roll my eyes. If M
looking.

The lady smiled. "What are *their* names?" she asked Mom.

"Boo and Gwendolyn."

"How cute." The lady peered at them. "How do you know which one is which?"

"Boo has on yellow socks today," Mom said. "Gwendolyn has blue."

Now *I* smiled. Boo *had* on yellow socks today and Gwendolyn *had* on blue. Before I changed them.

"They are so darling," the lady said.

Everyone thinks the twins are darling. On Halloween Mom fixed them up to be Raggedy Ann and Raggedy Andy, and everybody, *everybody,* said how darling they were. Some people said I was darling, too. I was a fairy-princess ballerina bride.

Boo and Gwendolyn need two people
to watch out for them all the time. Mom
says I'm such a big help. She doesn't know
what she'd do without me when Dad isn't
around. I don't know either. She'd be
really, truly overwhelmed.

One day we went to the beach.
Boo ran in the water in one direction,
and Dad ran after her. Gwendolyn
ran in the water in the other direction,
and Mom ran after her.

Who was left to run
in the water after me
if I ran in the water,
that's what I want
to know.

"If only there weren't two of them," I tell Dad. "If only they weren't girls. I used to be your only girl. I used to be special."

Dad's braiding my hair. "You'll always be my special big girl," he says. "Boo and Gwendolyn will be my special little girls." He pins my hair up to look like cats' ears. It looks good. "Miaow," I say.

The twins each have two teeth. They're good biters.

In the bathtub they bite their plastic ducks, and their sponges and each other. It's hard to believe what they can do with only two teeth.

They have lots of toys . . . two monkeys, two bears, two lambs, two horses. Dad says they could start their own Noah's Ark.

Their favorite toy is Mom's plastic laundry basket.
They sit in it.
They sit under it.
They push it.
They pull it.
They bite it, too.

Boo and Gwendolyn laugh even when nothing's funny. So we laugh with them.

At night, when they wake up, they don't laugh. They rattle their cribs and h

This morning the lady next door came to complain.
"Your twins woke me up last night," she said.
Mom apologized. "I'm sorry."
"Can't you keep them quiet?" the lady asked.
I scowled at her. "Babies *have* to cry." Who
does she think she is, picking on our
twinnies? Her rudeness
overwhelmed me.

Tonight, when Boo and Gwendolyn cried,
Mom and Dad carried them into their big bed.
I woke up, too, so I brought my pillow and
tagged along behind.

"Mom?" I whisper into the silence. "Dad?"

"Climb in, Sweetie," Dad says. "There's
room for all of us."